TIME TRAVEL EXPERIENCE

JOHN LOK

Contents

Preface

Introduction

This story is one scientist invents one time machine to bring whose one student to go to future time journey. It is my first science fiction novel written and a science comedy, a time travel science story. This scenario of this series takes place in four stages of journey.

The first journey indicates the Boston University lecturer, Jim's time travel machine invention and who invites the student , Johnny to enter this big circle time machine to go to future time travel together.

The second journey indicates Johnny go to the future court judgement journey alone. Johnny will meet himself in the future Boston city US court in the future time.

The third journey, the time journey traveler Johnny who will enter the time machine to discover whether who will do what kind of job in Boston University.

The end of story final journey, he will describe who is one human development science subject lecturer and he can see himself who is teaching in one large lecture hall as well as who can listen what his is teaching in the lecturer hall. Thus, he will know what he will teach and he will write all notes to remember to prepare his teaching in the future.

This time machine science story concerns one lecturer invents one time machine to help the main actor his student Johnny to catch his time machine to go to the future time and go back the present time travel. His student Johnny's surprising journey will be described in this fiction. This time machine journey story will describe the lecturer' Jim whose student Johnny time machine traveler how who sees the whole teaching process in Boston University teaching hall and he also listen what who is speaking about the one lesson of content of the human development subject in the Boston University hall in the future time in their final future time journey.

For his teaching content, he will listen who will teach about this topics concern global health factor, environmental factor, human security factor, economic growth factor, psychology factor and reproductive technology factor how which have close relationship to influence our next generation will grow in good or bad environment to alive.

So, the final stage will describe how the student Johnny who can know whether he what that who will teach whose students in the Boston university teaching hall.

In this story, you can enjoy to enter this time machine journey to arrive future our earth's or space's different places to do this future time research of scientific vision with student Johnny together. Also, you shall discover more surprising matters with Johnny after the student Johnny disappears in present time and his lecturer, Jim meets him in the future time. You will know whether how who solve the challenges in his next future different time journey.

This book is suitable to any readers who have interest to research whether time machine can be invented in the future. This is one time machine journey invention to concern the lecture Jim and whose student Johnny what who is experiencing in different places trips from this time machine invention.

Acknowledgements

Story characters
Time Traveler: Johnny, lecturer Jim's student, main actor
Time Travel Machine Inventor: Boston University lecturer, Jim, main actor
Future Judge and past prosecutor professor: Paul, actor
Narrator : alien Mary, actress
Boston university 2050 year human development science students and the future human development subject lecturer: time traveler, Johnny

Prologue

Table Of Contents

1

Travel machine invention

This story occurred in April 20 , 2020 year : 465 days later. One day, The Boston University lecturer, Jim met four students to discuss time traveling machine invention at dinner in one restaurant in Boston city . The Boston University student, Johnny who should be this lecturer's time traveler to do this time traveling experiment and he is showing to invite these other three students to show a model of a time machine invention. He says to them:

" Our Boston University lecturer, Jim has designed the time machine to help me to disappear in present time and I can go to future any times to travel. I invite you go to my lecturer Jim's laboratory to see how I can be disappeared from this time machine next evening at night time please."

Following, the next evening at night time, these three students arrive late again for dinner at this restaurant with Johnny together, then, Johnny brings these three Boston University students to go to his lecturer, Jim's Boston University laboratory with dusty and tried with a strange story to tell and attempts to do this time travel experiment to let them to see later.

After they arrive Boston University lecturer, Jim's laboratory. The student Johnny speaks to this small group of three interested students to sit in his lecturer Jim's laboratory to listen this strong story from his lecturer, Jim's speaking. Initially, the time traveler , student Johnny informs his these three student guests that they ought have to abandon some of their scientific and mathematical assumptions in order to follow his friend lecturer Jim's idea and his lecturer Jim also give an example from mathematics to explain this time travel invention before he enters this time machine to do this travel journey experiment. Then, this time machine inventor, Boston University, Jim who opens the door quietly to enter this laboratory. He explains his invention to let these four students to know. He says

"In general, most mathematicians acknowledge three dimensions of space, length, breadth, and thickness. However, my time machine invention has proved there is a fourth dimension, it is the dimension of time. Although, others argue that time can't be a fourth dimension because it can't be altered, because we can't change where we are in time, the time traveler. So, my student, Johnny will be dramatically claimed to do this time journey experiment with a time machine that will bring him to go to travel in time. Before I am a research assistant at Boston University, accidentally invents a time machine when attempting to construct a calibrator to measure the relationships between gravity and light. Unfortunately, it will only travel forward, to the future, in ever-increasing intervals of 12x. Hence, today, I invite you come to my laboratory to see my new time machine invention and let you to see my student, Johnny to do his time journey experiment. During this experiment, you will see how my student Johnny to be sent a bottle half a second into the future time by my new time machine, then he desperately shall take over the time machine, turns everything up to maximum and sends his one cigar three seconds into the future, burning out the circuitry in the process. Hence, my experiment shall prove to let you believe that the time machine must return to the present, a moment after departing, before going to any other future time. As a consequence, time used in the present day is lost forever. Hence, this time machine can only go to future time, but it can not go back past time from present time. "

After he explains his concept of this time journey experiment to let his students to know, the lecturer Jim takes a size of a large clock. His all four students audience, includes his time traveler , student Johnny give their full attention to see their lecturer, Jim uses whose psychologist's hand to press a button of the time machine. The four students discuss whether it went into the past or future.
" Is this a scheme to fool them? "

Then, The time traveler, Johnny takes them to go to his lecturer's laboratory to reveal a full sized version of the time machine, it is a large circular metal steel manufacturing thing, then every student attempts to enter this inside central empty black hole from this time machine following easily . At the same time, lecturer Jim also announces to say to them

" I plan to use this time machine to travel in time!".
Then, all are making speculation and joking, the four student guests laugh their student friend , Johnny. Then, the lecturer Jim says to his student Johnny

" Dear student Johnny , I permit you attempt to enter this time machine to enjoy your trip into the future from central metal manufacturing circular big empty black hole after I press the button to move this circle hole circles to exceed the light speed, then you can disappear in our laboratory and you can arrive future one point of time suddenly and I also had known my dear student Johnny student is my future research assistant to assist me to carry on time traveling experiments in the future, my other three students, have no chance to follow this student, Johnny to enter my time machine in the future."

Suddenly, Boston University lecturer Jim is stopped by a surprise visitor his student, Johnny who is standing front of him in laboratory. Jim bring him and these three students to go to see this time machine in his laboratory, it is a large metal circular shape thing which has high heights and long width to let any adults to enter its inside metal circular hole easily. Then, the lecturer Jim starts to press the button, then the metal circular black hole thing starts to circle faster speed, then it circles very fast to let these students to feel it is possible to circle to exceed light speed after Jim pressed the stop button. His student Johnny feels wonder about what will happen after he pressed the button immediately. Jim says to his student Johnny and the other three students immediately, Jim says " if any one entered my time machine to go through its central metal black hole after it's central metal black hole circles to exceed the light speed, the person will disappear in my laboratory and he will go to the future any point of time in the future place in our earth immediately. However, my time machine can not go back past time is its weakness, but, it can go forward unlimited future time is its strong point. So the actions of any characters can not have changed the past because the past is what their actions brought about. For example, one could not go back in time and kill one's grandfather because the time traveler would not be born."

When, these students was listening to this lecturer, Jim .Then, Jim also talks to his student Johnny again, who says

" You will be my only one future research assistant to assist me to do any time journey experiment from this new time machine, so you are one important person to assist me to carry on time traveling experiment to attempt to solve it's weakness and I shall wait you help me to resolve to stay in the past until all is done. So, why I bring you to see my new time machine in Boston University laboratory".

Now, student Johnny and these three students realize how this time machine can be completed in time by Jim's explanation. Once any people return to the present time from the future time, who can take as long as necessary in future time, then jump back to before the deadline with the future time again. Hence, these students believe this time machine can be go back present time from future time, although lecture Jim only talks to them to explain this matter will be occurred possibly ,but it has no any one has attempted to do this time journey experiment before. However, student Johnny has dream to go with his lecturer Jim to enter this time machine to carry on time traveling to prove whether his experiment is successful, but lecturer Jim refuses to say

" Sorry, dear student Johnny, I can not follow you to enter this time machine because I need to control this time machine's time to press the button to assist you come back present time any time after you arrive the future time's destination if you felt dangerous and you need to come back suddenly. Please believe me, you can come back safely if I could stayed to press the button to control this time machine metal black hole thing circles again, then you can come back present time to see us again. In fact, this accidental time machine is a adult height of mental circle shape with an oak base that was originally created to be a calibrator, but something malfunctioned in another dimension and caused it goes to time travelling when the person enters the large circle shape when the reset button was hit to make the circle shape mental is moving by light speed. It travels roughly in exponents of 10.3 degree of the button level only in a forward direction. It is not capable of being duplicated, and appears to be unique."

After the student Johnny listened his lecturer Jim. Then, the time traveler Johnny says to his lecturer Jim

" I have confidence to attempt to enter the inside empty central metal circle black hole from this large clock steel manufacturing time machine to carry on this time traveling experiment, I am waiting ,please Jim starts."

Then, Jim presses the button to push the large metal clock to circles the metal black hole , the hole circles fast. After 10 minutes, the black metal black hole speed circles to has been exceeded the light speed fast .These three other students also see the large clock time moves quickly forward . After more ten minutes, the lecturer Jim speaks

" You see this large metal black hole circles its speed has been exceeded the light moving speed. Do you feel this time machine 's circular speed has influenced my laboratory's environment which temperature falls down from 15 degrees to be below than 0 degrees in my laboratory? So why you feel cold in my laboratory suddenly, and the large metal black hole circles to change my laboratory's light to be dark , such as at night time, so you can not see anything suddenly during the time machine metal black hole circles after twenty minutes. O.K. now, my student Johnny can enter my time machine to send to arrive to the future any point of time of destination please, The most important point, you need to remember, you need to touches any wall at any building and you feel the wall has empty hole, then you can jump to the empty hole to come back because I had confirmed that my time machine clock has run to arrive the 15.5 hours of space standard time , after you can choose to come back present time again. So, I need to stay in this time machine to find when this time machine clock will arrive the 15.5 hours space standard time to press the button to circles its black metal circular thing to arrive to exceed the light speed again, then you can come back safely please, but it has one weakness, I do not know when the clock arrives the 15.5 hours of space time, it is possible that it is after one week, two weeks or three months. So, you must take care your safety in the future time and you need to attempt to touches any wall when you plan to come back any time please. However, when you plan to come back your present time of place from your future time of place and you need to know that it is only one time chance during you plan to come back your present time of place. So if you touches the wall first time, then you feel the wall is empty , but you choose not jump to the wall, then you need to wait the empty hole is the wall at least one week please ".

Then, Johnny says

" dear lecturer Jim, I believe you need me to revise analysis from my travel journey experiment. I also believe that lecturer Jim and me, our relationship is not one of lords and servants, but of livestock and ranchers. Hence, I believe that you must take care my safety after I am disappeared in present time by your time machine. Owing to you theorize that intelligence is the result of and response to danger; with no real challenges facing , I shall loss the spirit, intelligence, and physical fitness of humanity as its peak in this time machine journey, so I decide to attempt to enter this time machine to help you to carry on time travelling of journey experiment."

After Johnny entered this time machine, deducing that Time Traveler Johnny has taken his lecturer Jim 's time machine, he explores the secret tunnels, learning that due to a lack of any other means of sustenance.

Now, the other three students and the lecturer Jim have spent five hours to wait this time machine will stop to circle in lecturer Jim's laboratory and this time machine stops suddenly. At the moment, lecturer Jim press the button to control this time machine circles to achieve to exceed light speed again suddenly. Then, a man looks straight into their eyes, laughing and showing no fear whatsoever. This man is walking to come back from the time machine empty metal big black hole. These four students recognize this man is their student friend Johnny. They feel happy to see Johnny come back. Johnny seems to feel tried and he sits down on the chair and they give him a drink. After Johnny drinks, the lecturer Jim asks Johnny whether where he had gone within the five hours. Then, Johnny says

" dear lecturer Jim , I shall begin to speak my time journey to let you and your three students to listen please."

2

The time machine of future court judgement journey

Johnny begins to speak his time journey. After I entered this time machine, I explored the secret tunnel, learning that due to a lack of any other means of sustenance. I can not see any thing because it is very dark. I felt that I was passing one secret tunnel to through different things, due to these things are moving to exceed to light speed and this secret tunnel is very dark and it has no light, so I can not see what these things are. Suddenly, I felt that my body was passing through the wall to enter one building. I do not know where it is, but I believe that it is court.

However, after I had passed the wall to feel that I has entered one court place and I saw many audiences who saw me in the court. I was arrested by two policemen at the court. Then they bring me to sit on one chair in the court. One man sat on the central chair , who says

" Now, I am your judge and prosecutor and I am also your past Boston University's professor, my name is called Paul. You was charged one crime at this moment."
Then, I ask Paul whether what kind of crime that I had done please immediately.

Then, prosecutor Paul begins to tell what my crime was to let me and the audiences to listen to know whether what had happened to me in this five hours before I arrived this court. The judge, Paul tells me

" In the past, I was your professor in one Boston University in USA, you are my student from 2020 year. Then, I left my position of university and I decided to do a judge in 2025 year. Unlucky you were charged one crime on Sept. 20, 2023 year. Forward a few months, you were arrested for the alleged murder of a drug dealer who actually had a heart attack when he witnessed your appearance on one street in Boston city. Hence, you were charged to allege murder of a drug dealer . Do you commit to allege murder to heart attack to this drug dealer on Sept. 20, 2023 year."

I only know that I was entering the time machine to go to the future court. Hence, I answered to him to say
" I do not know what has happened to me and I believe that I have not kill the drug dealer on the street on Sept. 20 2023 year please".

Then, one man entered the court, I recognize who was familiar. Johnny says
"Dear lecturer Jim , do you know who was?" Then, lecturer Jim asks him
" I do not know , please you say to let us to know." Johnny say
" The man who entered the future court, who was yourself, lecturer."

Under in the circumstances, the time traveler Johnny is seen by his advocate or judge Paul . Paul has been given five days to travel into Johnny's past, and without revealing his true identity, convince his younger self to make a different choice at a beginning point to effect a different outcome for example, by quitting smoking, or choosing a different job. However, Prosecutor Paul is as advocate to play the role of judge. Hence, the judge Paul will give chance to let Johnny to change his future life again within the five future time travelling days together.

Then, lecturer Jim asks him why himself will appear in the future court. Johnny says

" I was shortly bailed out by you, you are the future lawyer and you can only be come from the future, and is left a note urging me to depart in the time machine quickly."

After you bailed out me to leave the court, I saw the one big black hole circles at the outside court wall fast and I could not touch any thing on the black hole because it was empty on the wall, then I attempted to enter this black hole and I was through one secret dark tunnel . I did not know how long time that I spent in the black hole, but I felt I spent five minutes in the black hole. Finally, I felt that I arrived one dark environment to walk to through this laboratory wall to enter this time machine to see you again. However, I feel horror because I do not believe that I shall kill any person in the future.

Nowadays Boston University lecturer Jim believes that he was possible to be one lawyer continues forward after time 5 years and upon re-materializing finds that his research assistant Johnny will be probable one killer in 2025 year. However, he hopes Johnny to enter the time machine to attempt to prove whether who will be one killer on Sept. , 2023 year. He asks Johnny

" Do you want to prove you are not the killer on Sept., 2023 year please?"

Then, Johnny answers to him,

" O.K. I accept to attempt to find whether I had killed this person or not on that future day".

Then , they see Johnny jumps to the time machine after his lecturer Jim presses the button to operate the time machine again.

This is the second time travel journey, the time machine shall bring Johnny to go to one future different place on the future one day, unlucky, it is not the date of the 20 Sept., 2023 future day. In fact, Johnny believes that the arrival date is 2252 year: 232 years later. Because he discovers his watch time record is 2252 year , 11:00 AM . Hence, he believes that his lecturer Jim has no ability to control this time machine to help him to go to the future day on 20 Sept., 2023 year exactly. However, The time traveler, Johnny appears in the middle of a stadium and there has one notice in the noticeboard called the

" Boston University research assistant, Johnny Korea Fuller sports Centre who is represented of this University founder".

The society is fairly futuristic (with trends like facial scarring), but the future Korean do not fully understand the time machine. However, scientific theories are being rewritten because of Johnny's time machine. Moreover, the time traveler Johnny also finds himself by the different new world place in a theocratic society. There had been an event billed as the Second Coming of Jesus, followed by a nuclear civil war between those who believed its veracity and those power in the Asia country, Korean. History had essentially been erased and restarted. The locals refer to the 2023 year is as Johnny's ages of 71 years old of the notice board in

"American Boston University of research assistant named Johnny is represented of this founder Korea Fuller sports Centre built in 2023 year.".
Hence, Johnny believes that he arrives the future Korea country and he is famous to represent his Boston University founder to build this sports center in Korea in 2023 year, but he does not know why he is 71 years old because it is future one day after 2252 years from 2020 present years. He think that it is possible the difference is between space time and earth time to cause his space journey time spent is very short time, but it's earth time is spent very long time. Then, Johnny finds one wall on Johnny Boston University founder Korea Fuller sports Centre, which appears one big black hole again and he touches it is empty, so he jumps to the big black hole again immediately. He hopes that he can go back his lecturer Jim's laboratory and he also feels fear that he could not go back to his lecturer Jim 's laboratory again.
This is his third time travel journey, unlucky, it again brings Johnny to go to one strange house which is firing after he jumps out from the house wall. It is a horror house because Johnny feels very dangerous, who falls down on the kitchen in the house. The house is very small , so the fire is close to the kitchen very quickly from the door. He also feels hard to breathe because it has no any air inside the house and all windows are closed. He fears that he will die soon.

Suddenly, he listens very loud outside the door. Then, he sees one firefighter damages the door to enter this house and says
" anyone is there please."
Then, Johnny says loudly
" I am staying in the kitchen, please save me ."
Then, the firefighter runs to kitchen and Johnny is replaced

by the firefighter , but the fire fighter will be fired to hurt his body to be heated to die unlucky and whose death made Johnny himself lose his memory. Now, Johnny feels he is a reborn person , whose name is John is as much an firefighter expert as Johnny is a beginner. Note that in the stage third time journey, the passage to the afterlife is different from stages one and second. In two episodes of the second stage, you shall see the future court judge Paul is the Boston University professor and Paul is playing the role of prosecutor to charge Johnny to murder the drug dealer in the future court. Hence, Johnny will predict his life is saved by a fire fighter and who can influence him to choose to do one fire fighter, so it is possible that who won't decide to be research assistant in Boston University in the future time if the fire fighter saved him , but he also lost his life.

In fact, Johnny time traveler will be died in heart surgery on May 1, 2027 when the story was airing. However, lucky, Johnny will have the twice in a lifetime. Johnny follows an aspiring angel who for some reason, won't enter heaven, but is assigned to guide a man who died prematurely. The prematurely deceased, Johnny is the fire fighter in his second lifetime , is playing by the episode guest , who may choose from the afterlife to correct something that went wrong earlier in Johnny of his life. Hence, Johnny can predict to know whether what disasters will occur to influence whose future life unlucky, so he can attempt to avoid these disasters occur in the future lucky.

Then, Johnny leaves the fired house, who finds one big black hole on the outside house wall. He touches it and it is empty, so he attempts to enter the big black hole again successfully. It is his fourth journey, the time traveler, Johnny again arrives in what appears to be an alien's city outside the earth , another earth. The society is based on bartering, is focused on material wealth and there is no poverty or illness. It is highly futuristic/technological and is controlled by an entity called alien culture.

In the new narrative, Johnny sees his watch is 2 million and twenty seven years, 11:00 AM, the time traveler Johnny tests his device with a journey that takes him after one million year from present time , he does not know this place where is earth or outside earth where he meets many aliens, a society of small, elegant, childlike adults. They live in small communities within large and futuristic yet slowly deteriorating buildings, doing no work and having a frugivorous diet.

The time traveler, Johnny describes his final frightening attempts at time traveling , how he has seen the moon and sun rush across the sky. Then, he decides to stop, and lands in a strange world of sweet , but weak people who only eat fruit. Also, The time traveler Johnny reflects on the differences he has seen between the new world of the future and this world. There are no diseases, no unpleasant insects, no useless plants and no work. Suddenly, the time traveler realizes that he can not find the empty big black hole on any wall easily because he feels that his lecturer Jim time machine is missing to show 15.5 space hours at this moment. Meanwhile, time traveler, Johnny who saves an alien person narrator, named Mary when who sees her is drowning in deep sea as none of the other people take any notice of Mary. The alien narrator Mary who develops and innocently affectionate relationship with Johnny over the course of several days. The alien Mary brings Johnny to go to one large and many trees green forest, where Johnny who finds a fresh supply of matches and fashions a crude weapon against aliens, whom Johnny who must fight to get back to go anywhere to find and to touch any the empty big black hole from any walls inside the forest's building if who wants to go back present time to see his lecturer Jim. He plans to take the beautiful girl, narrator alien Mary back to his own time. Because the long and tiring journey back to Mary's home is too much for them both, they stop in the forest, and they are then overcome by aliens in the night, and Mary faints. The time traveler Johnny escapes when a small fire he had left behind them to distract the pursuing aliens are lost in the fire, and the Time Traveler Johnny is devastated over his loss.

The time traveler, Johnny explains to the narrative alien friend Mary . He says
" time machine is so concerned with the theme of that "time" is in the title."
The time in the time machine isn't last week or next year- that's time on a human scale. Time in the time machine is on a scale that's totally beyond anything human. This is geological or even cosmic time. When I am this time traveler's Boston University student Johnny jumps into the future, I am not watching the lifespan of a person, but the lifespan of a species or even the lifespan of a star. Thinking about time in this way involves looking at the long view, even through that long view moves people out of the spotlight. My past memory is a form of time travel to visit you , you are as future my one alien future friend, Mary. Now, Mary , you see me, I has entered my time machine circular hole to visit you from the past time's light speed.

The narrator, alien Mary wonders if the time traveler, Johnny will ever return and whether he will be has gone into the past or the future. His friend alien Mary, narrator feels sadness that the time traveler, Johnny's hopes for mankind may be wrong. The narrator begins to write to record the traveler's lecturer has gone to his weekly dinner

guests that time is simply a fourth dimension, and his demonstration of a tabletop model machine for travelling through it. He reveals that he has built a machine capable of carrying a person through time, and returns at dinner the following week to recount a remarkable tale, Hence, the alien , Mary accepts to become the new narrator to serve her friend Johnny. Then, alien Mary asks him
"You mean that I am your future world friend. Are there other ways of time traveling without machinery or magic? "

Then, the time traveler, Johnny also explains to his future friend alien Mary again. He says
" since in the time machine is not just about making awesome machines that travel through themes: Technology and modernization , rather science is about a way of thinking . My future friend alien Mary, now you are my narrator, I need you help me to start with this observation, come up with a theory, test that theory and repeat as necessary until you're reasonably sure that you have the right answer to ensure that you have seen me on this day for your future day written record. Hence, when you see me in the future one day, I hope that you can give me any ideas to answer these questions to let me know, such as: What experiments does this time traveler, Boston University Johnny carry out in the future? What sort of experiments does Boston University student Johnny who talk about doing? What sort of tools do you think who takes with him when he decides to use the time machine?"

However, Mary is killed and a fire is lit by one alien. The time traveler, Johnny spreads throughout the forest, killing some of the aliens. Later, the time traveler Johnny finds one big black hole inside one house's wall in the forest, but it is a trap set up for him by the aliens and he has to fight his way out. Lucky, The time traveler finds one empty big black hole on the wall in one house wall near to him in the forest , so he enters the empty big black hole to escape to enter the time machine again.

The aliens know any wall 's empty the big black hole can help who to leave the present place and it is probable that he can enter the black hole to capture the traveler, but they do not understanding that he will use it to escape. The time traveler Johnny reattaches the levers before he travels further ahead to roughly 250 million years from his own time. In this fifth journey, there he sees some of the last living things on a dying Earth. Surprising like creatures slowly wandering the blood-red beaches chasing enormous butterflies in a world covered in simple vegetation. The time traveler, Johnny continues to make short jumps through time, seeing Earth's rotation gradually cease and the sun has no any heat to make the earth to be warm.

After Johnny arrives this future 250 million years world, he feels safely. Because he can not find any aliens at the moment, the time traveler Johnny begins to communicate with aliens are hampered by aliens' lack of curiosity or discipline, and Johnny who speculates that they are a peaceful, communist society, the result of humanity conquering nature with technology, and subsequently evolving to adapt to an environment in which strength and intellect are no longer advantageous to survival. Hence, Johnny believes that the future time 250 years is one safe environment to provide human to live.

Johnny, time traveler had spent longer time in some of this strange future place. Johnny says
" as soon as I got comfortable, I am off again to the next one. I hope to see my journey's friend lecturer and my student friends at this future happy strange place together, Jim stays longer in the future theocracy (where Jesus literally

rules) and the future (for back of a better word) as they both held a lot of promise. I feel this final trip was one -way and if I and my friend lecturer Jim and my student friends were return to the past (something that was quit broadly suggestive to have happened) I had to encounter something capable of reversing the process. I guess it all seemed to end rather abruptly where that point was concerned."

However, after this time, Johnny can not go back his lecturer, Jim's laboratory again. Hence, his present friends were waiting due to one week because his lecturer, Jim can not control the time machine clock to spend to arrive 15.5 space time hours easily to assist his student Johnny to come back to see him in his laboratory again successfully. They feel very sad and disappoint at this moment. Finally, lecturer , Jim hopes that he can attempt to enter this time machine to meet his dear student Johnny in any future point of time when this time machine clock shows the 15.5 space time hours spent standard on day. So, now he is waiting this 15.5 space time hours clock record in this time machine in the future one day.

3

The time traveler disappear journey

The time machine specifies either the exact time or the exact location to which the student, Johnny will be sent, (this limitation is similar to the time travel uncertainty principle). Hence, lecturer Jim feels difficult to assist his student, Johnny to come back present time easily. After many years, due to 2071 year, one day, Johnny's friend lecturer Jim discovers the time machine clock shows the 15.5 space time hours. Hence, he hopes that he can attempt to enter this time machine to meet his student , Johnny happily. Then, January 1, 2072 year: Johnny's friend lecturer Jim attempts his first time jump to the time machine to stay 31 days. Then, the lecturer Jim appears in the middle of the street, still in USA city Boston. He is then arrested for murder and grand theft auto. He is bailed out of jail by a Professor, Paul (Jim's Boston University professor in the mid 21st century) is actually lecturer, because Jim's descendant. Hence, Jim can predict who will die and he will be arrested for murder and grand theft . However, he doesn't know why he dead to be decendant in the future.

Then lucky, he touches one empty back hole in one wall of the street, lecturer Jim jumps in the black hole to go to another short time journey is going to future 320,000 years more later. Travel to the moon because there is no life left on Earth. There is only a strange mechanical creature there when who arrives . Lucky, Jim discovers Johnny stays to live in this strange place. At this point, Johnny and Jim begin to receive future email messages from future versions of lecturer Jim himself , and the aliens naively mistakes them to be from Jesus. The aliens warn Johnny and Jim whose willingness to sacrifice their lives in pursuit of these two earth people's goal, and the aliens advise them to stall for time to allow the future time traveler Johnny to catch up. On day, the lecturer Jim and his student Johnny accompanied one alien to go to one wall's empty black hole, begin to travel further and further into the future, discovering radically altered futures and entirely new species of intelligent life, including new species of animals evolutions of humanity and a race of intelligent bears.

After a confrontation where Jim and Johnny both narrowly avoid being killed by the one alien, they meet the other aliens who have been sending them future email messages . These beings send Jim and Johnny back in time, when allowing the one alien to continue jumping forward in time. The society is dominated by religious fervor. The Johnny time traveler is discovered as being uncircumcised (something that is mandatory in this new and strictly Christian-dominated society-and the time traveler Johnny, who is an assimilated Jew, did not undergo it). Johnny must attempt to go to into the future once again, now accompanied by his friend lecturer, the time machine inventor, Jim if they hope to go back present time together.

The time traveler Johnny and his friend lecturer Jim arrive several thousand years in the future again, Just outside Boston city , in USA country, in a society where all of humanity is wealthy and satisfied to a point to complete apathy. It is here that they encounter an artificial intelligence that controls Boston outside cities. These cities are curious about her own mortality, and having learned about Jim's time machine from historical records. In fact, the future time traveler, Johnny visits are more commentaries on present day societies, rather than his friend lecturer, Jim trying to predict what the future will actually be like. But the science sounds good, and using other worlds to comment on one's present is a device with roots that go back to America country, Boston city and probably further.

Nowadays, The time traveler Johnny and his friend lecturer Jim arrive 2025 year in the future again, Just outside Boston city , in USA country. Finally speaking, the time traveler, Johnny was squandering some great opportunities here. He was never in any one of these funhouse futures for long enough to get a real handle on things, to understand why and how the world developed this way. He would have been most intrigued to glean a better understanding of events that led directly from his past to the formation of the 23 RD century theocracy. After Jim discovered time machine, who had ever bought his friend Johnny went to their future time to find whether who had children or none in the future Boston city time. However, their one time machine journey went to their the date of current time twenty years later, their time machine let them to know their both will have several children and their future wives wish to join them on a journey to go to their current time from the future time when they met their wives, but they discover their future wives should be killed to die by heat death of the universe of this time machine. Hence, they do not decide to bring their wives to go back their nowadays time because lecturer, Jim is afraid it is possible that their wives will be killed to die from this time machine possibly. The reason is possible that their wives are future people, who are not nowadays people. Hence, their wives are sad to see their future husbands to leave them to go back nowadays time from the black hole of time machine in the wall at their house.

Finally, the time traveler , Johnny decides to go forward in time alone after he leaves his lecturer Jim in future Boston city. The Earth has stopped moving and he is on a beach and crabs start to attack him, so he goes forward again. The sky is black and there is snow. He manages to get back home where his friend lecturer, Jim's laboratory and his friend lecturer Jim doesn't believe his encountering because he had found who has arrived future Boston city again. Hence, his lecturer Jim feel Johnny's time journey duty has been finished, who does not need to attempt to enter this time machine again in the future.

This book's final episodes are centered on Johnny individual who had reached the end of his life in on timeline, and due to time machine grows time journey until unlimited future time , and the world is falling silent and freezing as the last degenerate living things die out. However, they will feel the future Boston city unique life difference what which is changed to present Boston sity custom life. Next part, I shall describe that Johnny will discover who will be Boston University human development science lecturer to teach one lesson in Boston University hall in his final time machine journey.

4

Human development science lecture lesson journey

When the Boston University Jim sees his student Johnny come back from the time machine again in laboratory. However, when Johnny has already leaved this black hole. Suddenly, his lecture jim touch Johnny's hand and push him to enter the time machine black hole again. So, Johnny can not come back present laboratory in Boston University. He and Jim feel that who are flying in the black hole, who feel spend ten minutes in the cold and black hole of the time machine. After the minutes, the Boston University lecturer Jim and his student Johnny has finished whose time journey to arrive future USA Boston university place again after who caught the time machine to arrive the future USA Boston University location at the future time. When Johnny and Jim leave this time journey machine. Johnny looks his watch's time is 9:00 AM and date is on 13 June 2050 year. After who left this time journey machine, Jim and Johnny

are walking toward whose Boston university direction in the street. Jim and Johnny feel whose future Boston University has not changed any more and Boston city has not changes any more. Then, suddenly, lecturer Jim talks
" my dear student Johnny, sorry, I touch your hand to push you with me to enter this time machine to go to USA Boston university again. The reason is because this is our final time to enjoy this future time journey in this time machine. Also we are this time machine final traveler to enjoy this final future time journey as well as it is also our final time journey because we can go to the future time and we can come back present time at this once time only. So, it seems that we can catch this time machine to go to future USA Boston University and come back once time final limit chance. It means that we can not catch this time machine to go to future time anywhere again because this time machine can not catch us to come back present time again for next time in possible."

Then, his student Johnny listens whose lecturer Jim and says
" Dear lecturer Jim, I thank you give me chance to enjoy to catch your invention of this time machine to go to future different places any more before. Now, I feel satisfactory and surprising to see human's future and I also know whether what challenges I shall encounter and I also know how I need to solve my future challenges and I also know when and what danger will occur to influence my safety for my future life. So, it don't need to catch this time machine to find what I want again because I know much more of whether what future myself encounter is. However, I hope that i can know what I shall do in my Boston University on this day 13 June 2050 year."

Then, Jim says to Johnny, " Time machine can bring us to go to our future Boston University and you will discover whether what you are doing in our future Boston University at this time final time journey. I believe it must have reason to do this final future time journey decision. I hope you can know whether what will occur to you after we enter to our future Boston university at this moment please."

After who entered this Boston University, Johnny see one big lecture hall, then Jim says
" it is possible that no anyone is sitting in this lecture hall because it is quite quiet inside this lecture hall. However, we attempt to open this lecture hall door to enter this lecture hall to find seats to sit down to find whether there are anyone are sitting there."
After who opened this lecturer hall door, Johnny and Jim feel surprising because who can see many students are sitting on chairs and all seats are full in this lecturer hall. The lecturer hall environment is full of students, so who feel difficult to find any seats to sit down. Then, who close the lecturer hall door quietly. They decide to walk to the front of the lecturer hall to attempt to find any seats to sit down. Lucky, they find final two vacancy seats to sit down at the front right line. So Johnny and Jim believe that this final future time journey has already planned to keep final two seats to let them to sit down in this Boston university hall. All students and they are waiting one minute, suddenly who see one man who wears shirts and takes one book to walk to enter this lecture hall politely. When the man is walking to the front line to close to Johnny's body. Johnny feels surprising and wants to speak that why your face is similar to me. However, Johnny feels shy to loud speak because the lecturer hall environment is quiet. When

Johnny sees the man face is similar to himself is standing on the lecture hall center table. He feels that the person is reproduced himself as another person as one lecturer is standing on the lecturer hall center table . His lecturer jim is sitting with him and he sees his lecturer Jim is laughing to look himself and Jim says
" please you keep quiet to listen the lecturer what who will speak or teach because I ensure that you will be Boston university lecturer and the person is yourself as you are these students' Boston university lecture to teach them on this day 2050 year."

After johnny has listened whose lecturer Jim's talking, his emotion is from surprising to change clam attitude and who has no doubt whether who will do what kind of job in 2050 year. The lecturer's face seems very similar even whose face seems to be reproduced from Johnny face. Moreover, Johnny also feels the lecturer's whole body is reproduced from his body. So, Johnny begins to feel who will be the Boston University's lecturer in 2050 year. At the moment, he take several papers and one pen to prepare to write to record the notes from the lecturer's teaching immediately.

The future lecturer , Johnny begins to speak, who says
" Dear students, this is my first day to teach human development science subject at this Boston university lecturer hall. I shall explain some contents of these chapters clearly. So, I hope you either write some notes to record if you feel some important points of these chapters and to avoid forget these important points please."

At the same time, the time traveller Johnny looks at there are half of student numbers to take papers and pens to prepare to write these important points. After ten seconds, the lecturer says "ok, now I begin to teach you and I shall finish this lecturer within one hour please." Then, the future lecturer says

"Dear students, do you know what is human development mean? The study of human development provides a view of the wellbeing of a population. I think global health is one factor can improve human life development. There are many factors that interrelate to produce the high health status and human development standards to developing and developed both countries. Do you know what are human development concepts ? OK , I explain what Human development concepts are. The concept of human development can give a more accurate measure of the wellbeing at people within particular countries." OK, I shall use what human development concept means from economic view.

"In economic view, human development is related to the level of wellbeing of people and promoting an environment where people can lead long, healthy and fulfilling lives. The gross National Income (GNI) of a country, or average income. However, although economic wealth is associated either better health outcomes and improved well beings wealth is rarely distributed equally. Also human development is explained about much more income. It is about creating an environment in which people can develop to their full potential and leading production, creative lives according to human needs and it concerns about expanding people's choices and enhancing whose capabilities. In the range of things, people can be and do, having access to knowledge, health and a decent standard of living and participating in their life of their society and decisions affect whose lives. "

"Dear students, do you agree health factor is an important part of achieving human choice to lead the life whose value. In order to improve human development, human need to build certain capabilities and freedoms. Such as leading long and healthy lives, having access to knowledge, having access to resource needed for a decent standard of living, e.g. housing and a reliable food and water supply, participating in the life of the community, participating in the decisions that affect their lives. Because without those capabilities human development can't progress and many opportunities remain inaccessible."

Then one student stand up and ask the human development lecturer this question, who says
" dear lecturer, may I ask you this question?".
The future lecturer says
" Of course, you can ask me."
Then , the student says
" Is it possible to measure the level of any country?"
After, the human development lecturer thinks about ten seconds, then who says
" Measuring the level of human development of a country is impossible. Because there are many aspects of people's lives that need to be taken into account, and to collect all of those index of selected countries in 2005 year indicated that Norway, Australia, United Kingdom, Japan had very high human health development index; China, Mexico had high human health development index; South Africa, India, Indonesia had medium human health development index; Uganda, Niger, Pakristan had low human health development index. In order for human health development to continually improve, the initiative, policies and health strategies employed must be able to be maintained over a long period of time. Otherwise, of this don't occur, the current level of human health development may decrease for future generations. I also recommend

sustainability concept to solve this challenge. Substainability is defined as meeting the needs of the present without compromising the ability of future generations to meet own needs. This refers to meeting today's needs and planning the country's health growth without creating problems or depleting resources for future generations. It has three types of characteristics of developed and developing countries. First, it is economic sustainability. It relates to the capacity of future generations to earn an income and the efficient use of resources to allow economic growth to provide our health need over time. Developing countries often experience low levels of economic sustainability to provide their citizen's health need. Second, it is social sustainability . It relates to future generations having the same. It is utilised in a way that will preserve resources, such as human right, political stability in order to let poor people have effort or chance to accept health service as same to rich people in any developed or developing countries both. Third, it is environmental sustainability. It relates to ensure the natural environment is utilised in a way that will pressure resources into the future. So, any developed or developing countries can have enough resources to provide health service to satisfy people's medical need at any time. Thus, hospitals' human activities, such as doctors, nurses should use natural resources only at a rate that allows these resources to replenish to let any patients can get enough medical facilities for their health treatment for future generations any time easily."

Then another student also stand up to ask him this question. He says

" Do any health strategies can raise human development?"

Then, the human development lecturer says

"In order for a country to improve the health status of its population and increase the capacity for individuals to lead productive, creative lives in accordance with their needs and interests, strategies that focus how to cause of mortality are important. This strategy needs program must include the elements of appropriateness, affordability and equity. Appropriateness means implemented any health program addresses the specific needs of a targeted community or population in the country. It requires the donor country or organization to carefully consider the available date to ensure that the proposed health programs clearly address the priority concerns of the community. For instance, if a community has high mortality rates as a result of malaria, then a program aimed at improving access to insecticide-targeted nets and anti-malarial medication would be required health strategies must consider the social, cultural and political aspects of the community. For example, an health education program needs to educate why males in families are likely to attend school than females. Therefore, the related health strategy needs to focus on females and ways to encourage families to send their daughters to school. To ensure the appropriateness to implement. The key elements are needed to consider such as: involving the local communities in the design, implementation and evaluation of any health projects will empower hospital staff people, choosing the right aid to reach poor people. Programs must focus in providing health services and resources that meet the most urgent health or educational needs of local communities. Basic necessities, such as the provision of clean water and sanitation are important in developing a foundation for positive health outcomes and ensuring economic and environmental sustainability; focus on educating women.

Gender inequality continues to be on issue for many developing countries, women are responsible for the majority of agricultural and domestic work, including the care of children. When women are educated and empowered, who are better able to care and provide opportunities for children, focus on health education. Education is one of the keys to good health and human development. Because people are needed to be employed and have the income to access the resources required for adecent standard of living. Ensuring the affordability of programs is important at the individual, community and national levels, at helps ensure economic sustainability to health service need. In individual poor people levels, who are living in poverty don't have the money to access medical programs and resources in a user pays system. Therefore, organizations responsible for the implementation of specific programs must consider how who are to be funded, so that individuals are not required to pay. For government or non government organizations, must be provided to ensure that programs are offered free of charge of the country is to gain maximum health benefits. Improving health contributes to the achievement of human development and sustainability as individuals who are able to work and participate in society are more able to led productive and creative lives in accordance with needs increases, so does a country 's gross national income. This enables the country to provide much needed resources. Such as clean water, sanitation and health care. As a community level, providing services is often costly, and as a result, the local government may not be able to meet the cost. For a developing country to develop and implement economically and social sustainable programs, affordability of services and needs. In order for implemented equity programs with society, any people, such as young or old age, male or female, poor or rich people need have equity health treatment. Governments need to creat health policies that act to improve and protect natural environments in which to provide who to enjoy to use, e.g. safe water supply service. Aim to let the country people to have afford clean water to drink. In economic planning to provide health service, human development is the main concern of the developed and developing countries. Human capital is one of the factors affecting human development to health service supply and two main aspects are needed to concern, such as health education and health service supply. Improvement in health results in human capital increase. This increase will happen through capital health accumulation, health improvement to raise labor productivity. Then, human development will be encountered in different standard, different criteria for health care considered. The cost of governmental health expenses is same as government's spending cost on health education and medical human resources supply will improve quality and increase life expectancy, it will impact on human capital and economic growth which is affecting on human development. How government health expenditure has an impact on human development? This question is asked to correspond to the assumption that government health expenditure has a significant positive effect on human development. It is also assumed, it has close relationship between health expenditure and human development. Human development is multi-dimensional process that involves changes in people, social structure, public attitudes and national institutions. Development process is needed to be assisted from economic organizations and political and social systems. Human development is the process of expanding the real freedoms that people enjoy it to use any health service in our society. It is as needed to overcome the major factors for dependency, that are poverty and injustice, poor economic opportunities, including neglect of public facilities. Human development also means the process of expansion options for human that the most important of these include a long and healthy life, education, enjoyment of a good standard of living, more choices include political freedom guaranteed human rights."

Then another student stands up to ask this question. He says

" Can you indicated any two aspects of human development?"

Then the future human development lecturer explained that

" in fact, we can say that human development has two aspects: one aspects is related to human capabilities, such as improved health, knowledge, and skills and other aspects of their capabilities to the opportunities and benefits purpose, such as being active in political , social and cultural issues. This counts the people in the community and practice to the formation of human capabilities in areas such as health, knowledge and meet the basic needs and to create jobs and reduced pressure to work in our society. In year 2011 year by United Nations Human development Report, it indicated human development ranking is from the very high level to high level to average level till to low level index. As mentioned, human development index is included these components, such as life expectancy, the adult literacy rate and enrollment ratio in education levels and GDP per capita. So, it means that factor that may increase than parts, will lead to promoting human development. What is these components meaning? Mortality rates show improvement in health status and life expectancy. Thus, these is a close relationship between mortality rate and human development, per capita GDP is one of the index of human development, much higher growth rate in this variable represents the increase in GDP and increase in human development, and it shows the positive and connect relationship between those two variables. Nowadays, providing this better health services is one of the fundamental aspect of social and economic development. Health services can be considered as other economic commodity and a durable commodity. When adequate health inventory was reduced , the people efficiency in cost, this process is called depreciation of is lost, this process is called depreciation of health capital. Therefore the natural life shows that the depreciation period is happening. The individual health inventory will be the function of health expenditure. So, health expenditure includes public and private health expenditure, its components is funds needed for health services, including treatment and prevention, plan future services for families and predicted emergency feeding. I believe that health expenditure will improve human development through channel, such as economic growth, reduce mortality rates and improve the learning process, direct and indirect health can affect economic growth. Health promotion makes human capital increase through capital health accumulation and has direct effect on growth. Also, health promotion can raise labor productivity, due to reduced illness working days. It is possible to say that, health impact on the economic growth is due to health effect on labor productivity. As healthy workforce is more motivated and higher productivity . Usually the final efficiency is concerned the factors of production, such as land inventory, capital machinery, equipment and intermediate inputs and technology. Because more healthy people are more efficient with a certain measure of capital and probably the work done by them equal to patients. Economic growth is used as a representative and the display of social welfare. So, by the human development index, economic growth increases has also increased social welfare and human health development. Besides, improvement in health manpower, since the improvement of health conditions will increase the attractiveness of investment and education and training opportunities. Then human will be needed to further health education and skills. Therefore, increasing health expenditure will need human to improve ability to learn and increase motivation will promote human development to encourage to enter health industry career. As it explained, health expenditures with provides positive impact on human development through increased economic growth and reduction of mortality rate and improve the learning ability. It seems that government ought spend health expenditure, it will cause public health promotion and through specified channel will be to encourage human development to health industry career."

Then, another student asks

" Can you explain what factors can influence human development?"

After five seconds, the human development lecturer says

"Does environmental degradation affect human development and economic development? Economic growth will bring negative externalities, for example, environmental pollution. However, economic development is an increase in the real income per capita, as well as improvement in a variety of indicators such as life expectancy, welfare of the nation, quality of life and quality of environment. The rapidity of modernization, urbanization and industrialization has led to serious environmental concerns issues. However, economic and social changes, such as large increase in population, shift of population from rural to urban areas, increase in mechanized and chemical agriculture, industrial production, capital accumulation and technologies have transformed the county's natural resources, both as a source of factor inputs and as a by-product of pollution. Economic development and human development efforts are increasingly constrained by environmental concerns, including, degradation of forests and fisheries, lack of fresh water resource, and poor human health as a result of air and water pollution. Rapidly increasing population is one of the main obstacles in the way of economic development as well as human development. Over population explosion is not benefit to human development. Such as China could not slow its population growth rate, it would have not an easier job in dealing with like education, health, employment, housing, food, the environment etc. challenges, even Chinese people's life quality won't be improved. In the health, nutrition and education prime areas of concern of China will be worse or the worst to compare to the developed countries, e.g. America, England. If China will be still increasing over human over population development in the future. Another major determinant of economic develop as well as human resource development is urbanization, the share of urban population in total population. The rates of urbanization and its attendant impacts differ in regions across the global. In fact, Asia contains almost half the world's mega cities and continues to urbanize rapidly. The origins of may global environmental problems related to air and water pollution are located in these cities. For example, China, many transports, like cars, buses etc. are more intensively used in urban areas as compared to rural parts of the economy. Moreover, food and other consumer products have to be transported into cities, which again should lead to higher pollution that affect human health. The other sources of water pollution come from various other different situations which tend to occur in urban areas. For example, soil particles from construction and demolition sites, and also oil and toxic chemicals from car maintenance and run off from road surfaces. Such an urban lifestyle and an urban design are also factors contributing to water pollution. However, much of the sewage in urban areas goes untreated and is dumped into rivers and lakes. As a result, surface water and ground water have been increasingly polluted. However, in urban areas, education facilities are better than rural areas, in this case, urbanization affect human development positively. For example, urbanization in China plays the roles not only for improving human capital , but also for controlling over population growth. Due to over population human development will contribute poverty to China and it won't bring the best in human enterprise as well as the worst social services available in the country. Also, it will cause social ills to China, such as overcrowding, unsanitary living conditions, drug addiction, social unrest and environment pollution. It seems China needs to limit its over population to be increased every year. It won't earn the benefit from human development, Otherwise, it will bring disadvantages form over population. So, China government needs to concern how to control over population explosion. Human development can damage natural environment. Human impacts on land have global, regional and local consequences including changes in land cover, climate, atmospheric composition, biodiverity, soil condition and water and sediment flows . The rate that natural habitats are being lost and environmental processes are being altered is greater than past. Land use refers to the human perspective of how land is utilized (i.e. protected area, forestry for timber products, agriculture and human development). Land cover is the ecological state and physical appearance of the land surface (i.e. closed forests, open woodland, or grasslands). Why can human development damage nature environment if human neglect to concern to protect natural environment? Over the centuries two important trends are evident. First trend is the total land area dedicated to human what has grown significantly, and second trend is increasing production of products and service (mostly food and fiber) has intensified both use and control of the land (Richards 1990). Human decision and social drivers are fundamental forces behind learn cover change. According, social drivers like local and global economies must be considered when discussing land use and land cover change. For example, forest transitions was as a concept suggested amounts of forest change in predictable ways as societies experience economic development, industralization and urbanization for large size countries, such as America, England, Japan, France etc. developed countries. For example, tropical deforestation resulting form changing national and global-scale economic opportunities is a major contributor to global land use change. So the natural damage is caused by individual and public decisions largely result in agriculture expansion, wood extraction, and infrastructure extension, causing regional and local deforestation. The human development lecturer indicates. In the recent past, the rate of change of land transformation worldwide has accelerated. More acres of grasslands and forests lane been converted to other land cover types in the last from 1950 year to 1980 year than the past. Most quantitative assessments old land use change have focused on changes in metropolitan areas. However, exurban developments patterns have changed radically in the United States in the last 50 years. the first major shift occurred between 1950 year and 1970 year and was driven by urban growth. The majority of non-urban countries lost population to urban centers, when a significant number of people moved from urban cores to new suburban. For U.S. country natural damage example, the geographic extent of exurban land development in the U.S. is over seven times larger than that of urban and suburban development. When each individual lot is not necessarily ecologically detrimental, the cumulative effects can be problematic. So, U.S. country of the rate of land use change can be of ecological concern challenges nowadays. How can ecological impacts of land use to U.S. country? Ecological impacts of land use are wide-ranging and varied . Nearly all human issues surrounding land (settlement, forestry, conservation, sociology) involve its transformation and fragmentation. Thus, the modification of the relative abundances and spatial distribution of natural habitats and land cover types can affect biodiversity in distinct ways. The land cover change on biodiversity is change in population dynamics. Although U.S. is a developed countries, but it chooses to use land or forest to build many houses or offices or shopping centers or entertainment facilities one day. It will encounter nature land shortage challenge. Then, it will lack plants to produce oxygen to provide fresh air to human to absorb, even fishes will lack water to alive in river or ocean. Thus, human can not neglect nature environment protection issue when who need to live in anywhere. Exploring future impacts on environment constraints on human development. Environmental constraints are important consequences for human development. The possibility that such constraints, including climate change, an environmental challenge scenario, and an environmental disaster scenario. What can human developmental impact environmental damage? If natural environmental encountered damage. It will influence agricultural challenge, such as climate change will influence plant, fruit, rice production, reducing agricultural supply and consumption and trade of crops and meat, it also carries ocean fish catch supply reduction, less land use in crop, forest, urban and demand for food, for livestock feed, and for industrial use of agricultural products. Thus, human development has possible to influence climate environmental change to be bad, then bad climate environmental change will influence not enough farm and river supply numbers or poor natural water and land quality to provide human to grow up meats and vegetable and fish to supply for human eating. "

Then one student asks this question

" Why does human development influence environmental change to be poor?"

After ten seconds, the human development lecturer says

"The improvements in human development, incomes continue to rise, driven in part by technological advances and diffusion globally. Education and health levels rise as incomes improve and reinforce economic growth. Among such structural representations, human development will influence natural environmental protection, such as solid fuels for cooking, outdoor air pollution, and levels of access to safe water and sanitation all impact health. Also illustratively, temperature, precipitation and carbon fertilization change agricultural productivity and affect food production and undernutrition (it affects mortality in the short run and worker production through human developmental in the long run). Specially environmental challenge, it does capture it in some, such as fossil fuel use. There is no representation of radical technology advances or their uses, such as the widespread uptake of carbon capture and sequestration or dramatic shifts in artificial intelligence. The environmentally based and other challenges to human development. Considered most directly, environmentally based challenges generally involve either constraints with respect to withdrawals of biophysical resources from global sources or constraints with respect to the use of global systems as sinks for outputs from human ones. Often, as in the case of dirtying human own drinking water, who involve both. Similarly, in a world recognized as having plentiful capital and labor and , in fact, having difficulties putting both to productive use. Many of forces restraining economic growth are, at the core, tied to environmental systems. Advances in multifactor or total factor productivity depend on a wide range of physical, social, and human factors. Although, some environmental factors, notably energy prices, affect that productivity, the model almost certainly under-represents such impact, suggesting the need to include additional environmental constraints. "

Then another student ask

"Why has it close influence between human development and climate change?"

After five seconds, the human development lecturer says

" Human development had moved to beyond biophysical

challenges to social ones, such as environmental forces aging of population is a major concern and pressure moving forward for many wealthy countries. Many other social factors will challenge humanity when pressure of environmental constraints push human into competition for water, energy and land. However, it has uncertainties about the relationships between environmental variables and human development. How can human development create the environmental risk scenario? The scenario represents environmental risks at the household (indoor solid fuel use) local (water and sanitation), and global levels (especially increasing impacts of global warming on agricultural production). Nowadays, the environmental challenge scenario includes, all changes are relative to underlying dynamic values. For instance, an increase in fertility would be relative to underlying rates that are decreasing for almost all developing countries, lowers the rate of progress in cost reduction for production of renewable energy, positing impacts on yield from environmental factors not in the model, the scenario slows growth in agricultural yield by 0.5 % annually to a total of 25 %. Also reduces global supplies of fresh water by 25% over 50 years (0.5 % annually) causing the pollution effect of carbon dioxide on crop fretilization, with respect to health related issue, the scenario slows down progress towards improved and household connected water and sanitation by 50 % over 50 years and increase urban air pollution and indoor use of fuels by the same amount, poor health rate increasing, focusing only on HIV/AIDS directly increases the death rate globally from AIDS by 20% over 20 years slows down the peaking of HIV prevalence in sub-Saharan Africa by 8 years and increases the peak incidence in sub-Saharan Africa by 4%points. So, it seems human development can bring environmental disaster, such as overuse of fossil water and changing run-off patterns from glacial melting , progressive deforestation and land degradation, species loss and dramatic declines in biodiversity, accelerated incidence of extreme weather event. So, human peaking production of oil and gas and building etc. economic active damage will cause our natural climate change and will damage natural environment for our next generation live in the poor environment in the future. "

Then the human development lecturer drink one cup of water, then he asks whose students

" Why does human security need to be concerned to human development? Nowadays, security is need in response to the complexity and interrelatedness of both old and new security threats, from poverty to ethic violence, human trafficking, climate change, health, international terrorism, sudden economic and financial downturns . Also human security is required or a comprehensive approach that utilizes the wide range of new opportunities to fight such threats in an safe manner. So, it is a linkage between human development , human right and national security for future human safe life development. Because human needs freedom, safe, no threats situation to be survival, if human feel no freedom and safe, then it will influence human can not develop any technological innovation, education change, medical health, housing and social welfare to any country more easily. For example, economic security main threats include poverty, unemployment; health security main threats include deadly infectious diseases, unsafe food, malnutrition, lack of access to basic health care; environmental security main threats include environmental degradation, resource depletion, natural disasters, pollution; personal security main threats include physical violence, crime, terrorism, domestic violence, child labor ; community security main threats include inter-ethnic, religious and political security main threats include political repression, human right abuses. Thus, why human need to do protection. Protection implies a top-down approach. It recognizes that people face threats that are beyond their control , e.g. natural disasters, financial crises and conflicts. Human security therefore requires protecting people in a systematic, comprehensive and preventative way. Empowerment strategy means a "bottom up" approach. It aims at developing the capabilities of individuals and communities to make informed choices and to act on their own behalf. Empowering people not only enables them to develop their full potential, but it also allows them to find ways and to participate in situations to ensure human security for themselves and others. To human development's objective of growth with equity, human security adds the important dimension of downturn with security. Human security acknowledges that as a result of downturns, such as conflicts, economic and financial crises, ill health and natural disasters, people are faced with sudden insecurities. Therefore, in addition to its emphasis on human well-being , human security is driven of development gains. Thus, because human insecurity will cause bad influences to our societies. So, why human need to concern human security issue. Energy development is another security issue, human need to concern energy is deeply implicated in each of the economic, social and environmental dimensions of human development. Energy services provide an essential input to economic activity. They contribute to social development through education and public health, and help meet the basic human need for food and shelter. Modern energy services can improve the environment, for example, by reducing the pollution is caused by inefficient equipment and processes and by slowing deforestation. However, rising energy use can also worsen pollution and mismanagement of energy resources can harm ecosystems. Thus, the relationship between energy use and human development are extremely complex. Human need to concern sustainability of development, it can be assessed in economic , environmental and social terms. Energy sustainability requires meeting our energy needs upon which economic development depends, when protecting the environment and improving social conditions. Sustainable development is about finding acceptable trade-off between economic, environmental and social balance allocation goals. For example, an increase in energy input costs can be compensated by investing more in energy efficient technology, shifting to less energy-intensive production or using more labor, where it is in surplus supply to some countries. Hence, our governments have need to concern how to change in energy prices. In many poor countries, under-investment in public utilities, inefficient management, under pricing and a generally unattractive climate for private investment cause energy shortages and hold back economic growth and development. Hence, human need to concern how to allocate enough energy to supply to any countries to use or consume in the most reasonable energy price fairly. It aims to either reduce shortage energy challenge to some countries or surplus of energy challenge to some countries to provide different countries‘ people to use or consume fairly in our earth."

The human development lecturer says
" do you agree economic growth and human development close relationship?" Now, I shall explain their relationship. "Economic growth can reduce poverty and improving the quality of life in developing countries. Growth can cause prosperity and opportunity. Strong growth and employment opportunities can improve incentives for education entrepreneurs, even human development. But under different conditions, similar rates of growth can have very different effects on poverty, the employment prospects of the poor and broader indicators of human development. The extent to which growth reduces poverty depends on the degree to which the poor participate in the growth process and share in its proceeds. Future growth will need to be environmentally sustainable. Improved management of water and other natural resources is required, e.g. movement with low carbon technologies by both developed and developing countries. Some report indicated growth is the important method to help human to solve poverty. For example, a flagship study of 14 countries in the 1990 year found that over the decade, poverty feel in the 11 countries that experienced significant growth rose in the three countries with low or stagnant growth. On average, a one per cent increase in per capita income reduced poverty by poverty was particularly in Vietnam, where poverty fell by 7.8 % a year between 1993 and 2002 year, the poverty rate from 58% to 29%. Other countries with reductions over this period include India, Tunisia, etc. each with declines in the poverty rate of between three per percent and four per cent a year. Driving these overall reductions in poverty was the rebound in growth that began for most of the countries in the mid-1990 year. The median GDP growth rate for the 14 countries was 2.4% year between 1996 year and 2003

year (Adams, R 2002). The report also showed India has seen significant falls in poverty since the 1980 year rates that accelerated into the 1990 year. This has been strongly related to India's impressive growth record over this period. China alone has reached over 450 million people out of poverty since 1979 year. Evidence showed that rapid economic growth between 1985 year and 2001 year was crucial to this reduction in poverty. So, it implies the positive link between growth and poverty reduction is clear. The impact of the distribution of income on this relationship, in particular, whether higher inequality lessens the reduction in poverty generated by growth is less clear. The levels of income inequality are important in determining how powerful on effect growth has in reducing poverty. For example, it has been estimated that a one per cent increase income levels could result in a 4.3 % decline in poverty in countries with very low inequality or as little as a 0.6 % in poverty in highly unequal countries. To conclude, the report also indicated that growth does not necessarily lead to increased inequality. When some theoretical research suggests a causal relationship between growth and inequality, the consensus of the latest empirical research is that there is no consistent relationship between inequality and changes in income. Thus, it seems economic growth and human relationship has close relationship. Then, it will bring this question. Does human development influence the causes of global change? Global change may include: globalization, democratization, population growth, environmental protection, global crisis, commonly shared resources, poverty, social justice, information technological improvement, social capital and economic development, corruption, and moral economy, people centered development, sustainable development, individualism, mutuality, positive and negative peace and violence and security etc., these social issues influence. How does global change influence human development of educational, cultural, economic, technology, labor production etc. issues. However, we also face mankind limitations in dealing with the most important issue: the deterioration of our environment, social injustice, the widening gap between the wealth and the powerless, lack of mutual respect for diverse cultures, security and sustainable development. Dissemination of information can be considered the single most dynamic factor in human development. At the 21 st century, the whole world was aware that something extraordinary will be changed. The speed at what information now travels around the world changed fastly. This phenomenon can impact human development. For many globalization is connected will the speed of capital markets, or the location of sport shoe factories in places heretofore unknown. But globalization also rises in the adoption of Asian children by American parents, the growing popularity of international music, soccer in the United States and of basketball in Europe, Africa and Asia, the arising of international disputes before the public and the opportunity for public opinion to influence even military courses of action. Globalization of information, attitudes and values may change traditional culture difference to influence different countries. This rapid dissemination of information has resulted in globalization, a conflation of space and time to impact our traditional space of time of lifestyle. Globalization has been predominantly a Western phenomenon, but by the 21 St century, as electricity and satellite communications have spread ever more widely around the world, access to information and knowledge is freely available to increasing number of even poor and isolated population. Globalization and the dissemination of information are closely linked, but neither necessitates nor guarantees human development. Human development requires the transformation of information to knowledge and then to wisdom and moral behavior. The barriers to this transformation process, more difficult to change the colonization of space, more complicated than those that block the understanding of physics are neither technical nor economic in a primary sense. The centrality of knowledge to human development is evident to explore new knowledge can be put to use to moderate the world's population , how access to information can be democratized, how an informed world population impacts on globalization on environmental protection or peace and security. So, it seems global information can influence global human development will be improved or advanced in the future. It implies global information economic growth and human development which has close relationship to cause human developed in our past history."

Then, the human development lecturer says

" Now, I shall explain what the key themes in human developmental psychology to influence human development process is. Human development theories include psychological, social cultural, behavioral, biological and multi-level theories. Human developmental psychology theoretical perspectives may include, such as psychoanalytic learning, social learning, cognitive, biological, ecological aspects. Human need to know what our human development psychology mind. Because human can have correct human development behavior from correct psychology mind. Then we (human) can have more correct mind to decide how to prepare our future human development methods to let us to get the more correct benefits to give to our next generation. How can human do correct behavior? Human can observe or develop habits from observational learning experience, which depends on environment factor to decide to do correct human behavioral development of choice. Human development of learning methods include legitimized study, social cognition, educational performance training contributions. How does sociocultural influence to cognitive development? How is culture transmitted from our generation to next generation? In information processing viewpoint indicates human mind is like a computer, information flows in, is operated on, and is converted to output (answers etc.) . Contributions include human insights, filled gaps, approach to problems, correcting errors strategies: so, by nature, all human are alike, but by education, widely different . Hence, education is one important factor to influence human development in the future. Hence, the correct human psychological mind and development of human resources and economic development has close relationship. Because economic development is critical to all countries. Well managed economics include jobs and prosperity highly developed education, and health infrastructure; good governance; physical development; better quality of life; community and social development; equity with safety net for the poor and sick. Why is the development of human resources is important? Human resource development concerns education and training of a nation's citizens, so who are able to reach the full potential. It is a key driver and component of economic development, it can lead to number of social and economic benefits, including jobs; reduction in poverty; increase standard of living and better quality of life; better civil society etc.; ability and level of a country to invest in the education and training of its citizens will depend on a number of factors and development of people in developing countries is more conductive to economic development than investment in physical infrastructure. What is human development index (HDI): it means to measure the average achievements in a country in three basic dimensions of human developed (i) a long healthy life (ii) knowledge (iii) decent standard of living. There are three main categories of human development, when HDI below 0.5 , it is low human development; when HDI between 0.5 and 0.8, it is middle development; when HDI of 0.8 and above , it is high human development. For example, Africa, the scale of poverty is so hung for the majority of the Africa population, with basic needs priority of education, skill and other human resource cost, affording foreign direct investment is critical of economic development. However, I recommend Africa ought create conductive business environment for investment, ensures mutually beneficial for both the host county and other countries and ensures that foreign investment leads job and social and economic development. To conclude, human need have correct psychological mind and attitude to decide how to develop human resource to achieve economic growth aim. Otherwise, if human had not correct psychological mind and attitude, then human will have more chance to do any wrong decide to develop human resource to cause our economic threat in possible. Thus, I encourage human ought have good education to provide training to us to build correct psychological mind and attitude to develop efficient human resource to let our next generation to enjoy or consume in the long future time."

The human development lecturer begins to explain another reproductive technology factor how to influence human development. He says
"Human capabilities play an important part in the emergence from stagnation to modern economic growth. Will human development interacts with technological change cause a sequence of market failures? These dynamic intergenerational, human development traps male economic growth slower, stratified and transitional and social organization of the society of birth. The intergenerational nature of human development and the slow rate of transition that market failures in human capital investment impose, take on an important role. As a result, a low incentives for human capital accumulation, in which slow technological change leads to population growth without a resulting equilibrium rise in per capita income. A slow increase in the rate of technological change eventually makes this steady state unstable. It seems that slow technological change won't have an equilibrium with low life expectancy to one with high life expectation in which skills and knowledge making economic growth. As a dynamic conception of human development is what happened in stagnant countries once the leading countries developed? How does human development interact with economic growth? For example, China has over population human development crisis, it barriers in nutrition and health, and barriers to productivity growth, continue to occur in the present day. In China, it has experienced the stage between the lower peak and the upper peak with the life expectancy period of time. The lower peak life expectancy group has semi-stagnant life expectancy. The higher peak life expectancy group has high and improving life expectancy, when the middle peak life expectancy

group can be though to be in a rapid transition from semi-stagnant, low life expectancy to high life expectancy stages. However, it will bring disadvantages when the country life expectancy reaches the high life expectancy stage. It will experience a high productivity barrier if research and development implementation and semi-stagnation (a steady state growing at a lower rate than the leading edge technology) in the country. Due to the country will be experiencing low technology growth, but it has over population growth. It means the human capital accumulation change is more larger than high technology change. For example, China technology can't be changed to improve more than population growth, it 's medical technology can't be improved, then it will encounter food production shortage and lack of medical facilities and lack of nutrition and health improvement, lower income to rates of economic growth barriers to high productivity challenges. Those surely involve over population human capital accumulation in the form of lack technological skills and knowledge and lack technological change efficient economics and equality challenges in China. Can scientific development influence human development, such as DNA reproductive technology? Specifically, human must consider the complex relation of our progressive and increasing scientific knowledge of the world and its resulting technologies to what has up until now been our essential human nature. Can science and technology threaten human nature? Should human beings be entrusted with the power that science offers them? Have the age-old limitations on human power been a protection from our own capacities for destruction? One source for hope is the possibility that science. In the near future, may be able to change human nature itself. This may happen by either eliminating certain destructive traits or by enhancing others or it may occur because the abundance that technologies can offer human will make competition on larger necessary for human survival. The question of human nature, though abstract, is directly on humans' ability to imagine and plan for a future. Are there constraints placed on possible developments by essential components of human nature? However, human development are very far being able to formulate those questions satisfactorily, let alone provide a useful answer to them. Another difficulty that if we think that science can assist or improve or change human development, when human development is trying to anticipate what it will determine the shape and direction of scientific and technological progress. Science, of course, it is a factor to possess its own internal determinants of what direction it will take. Nature and the world is the another factor to provide human development. But, equally powerful ones are generated by politics, social and economics. It is important to remember that scientific and technological process, which seems to human, can be changed, redirected or completely stopped by changes in the culture. For example, DNA text was unknown. Today, human have gained the ability to manipulate this text almost at it will be in organisms, even as complex. In the next few years, our ability to do this will extend to humans. The easy choices are to improve our quality of life by reducing the costs and discomforts of the major diseases that today affect mankind. However, there may well be differences of opinion whether the ultimate goal is a life span or a more disease free existence at the current average life span. The hard choices are what human properties do we enhance and which do human leave as is. Should human enhance our capabilities, offer the capability for regeneration, produce enhanced condition, more efficient interfaces with computers and wireless communication ? In order words, natural selection no longer determines the evolutionary process, artificial selection does. As DNA technology is a sequence for some species and understand many of the rules. What will our knowledge and technology be like in fifty years? I hope technology e.g. DNA can be improved to skill diseases, such as skin cancer, cardiovascular disease, breast cancer, adult disbetes, osteoarthritis, lung cancer etc. human diseases. Thus DNA technology will have possible to solve human disease challenges in the future. In the near future, human will see the technology which depends on our knowledge of DNA combine with reproductive technology to give human reprogenetics, reproductive and genetic technology, which will be alike to ensure or prevent the inheritance of particular genes in children. In the past, many biologists doubted that genetic manipulation of the kind human are discussing ever be possible, primarily because of the infinitesimal sizes involved. Advances in technology, however, allow human to operate within acceptable risks. In fact, very soon reproductive technology will operate at levels of risk below that of natural sexual intercourse. Other doubts arise from religious and philosophical objections to reproductive technologies and involve ideas about the human development or hesitations about taking on responsibilities that traditionally have been left to drive power or the operations of chance. It is also only natural for parents to wish to endow their children with advantages, especial those that will affect their children's economic success in later life. There are several common examples of genetic manipulation that occurred long before the discover of DNA. As for mental abilities, it is unlikely that natural selection itself will change that, since smarter people do not have more babies. In fact, scientists don't really control technology. It is people and government who use scientists and determine low all those technologies will be used. DNA is at biotechnology, it seems that it has benefits to human, but it also has no moral acceptance to reproductive any animals or human function. Thus, human need to concern DNA technology whether it will be essential to continue to research for human development in the future. In conclusion, human need to concern whether how to improve human development, also it can reduce any disadvantages will influence our next generation live for long term in human future development as the same time. Because human development process will cause disadvantages to our environment and quality of life and technological development or innovation to influence human life nature change. So, we need to concern these issues for my next generation to let who have good life quality in the future."

Finally, the one hour of the future lecturer teaching time has arrived. The future lecturer says
" Do you have any questions to ask me please." He waits till to ten seconds, then who says" good day, thank you, you go to this lecturer hall to listen my first time teaching. My name is Johnny, if you have any questions after you go home to read today my lecturer notes. I invites you ask me any questions which concern today my teaching contents please."

The time traveller Johnny and Jim immediate to go to the front of lecturer hall to attempt to contact the future lecturer Johnny. Suddenly, the lecturer Johnny disappears in the lecturer hall. They look the lecturer Johnny's whose body slow disappears in the air from his head in the beginning , then whose two hands also disappear, next whose body also disappears, finally, whose two legs also disappear in the air. Suddenly, who discover one secret and horrify matter occurrence. they discover the whole lecturer hall's desks and chairs are disappearing by one to one from the first front line to the end line, till to all desks and chairs disappear all in the air. This disappearing processing only needs to spend about one minute fast speed. Then, who also discover the number of 100 students are also disappearing by one to one in the air. This disappearing processing also only needs to spend about one minute fast speed. Finally, who also discover even, the lecturer hall whole building is disappearing. In the beginning, the windows start to disappear, then the lecturer door, next even Johnny and Jim standing location of the front hall is also disappearing. Suddenly, who feel surprising, due to the whole lecturer hall environment changes light to dark environment, so who can not see anything. At this moment, Johnny and Jim feel to climb to the black hole to enter to the time machine again. In fact, they are jumping into the black hole through much light in the time tunnel. Again, after about one minute, they both see the light in the black hole tunnel and they feel whose close light flying speed is stopped and who can stand on the hard stones when who see light and jump away to the hard stones from the black hole tunnel. Safely, Johnny and Jim feel happy because who see their black hole time in laboratory.

Finally, in the end of this time machine journey, the Boston university lecturer, Jim says

" my dear student Johnny, I thank you like to join to me to participate on this different time of future time journeys. Now, you can know what your future life role is and what kind of job you will choose to do and you also know when you will encounter hurt, even die threat unlucky in your future some point of life time from these future time journeys. As one Boston university graduate student, you can feel that I seem to be your father to hope that you ought know how to plan your career in the right way. However, our duty of these time journeys have finished at this moment. I shall damage this time machine because it can't help us to come back present time, if we catch it to attempt to carrying on any time journey experiments to go to future times again. Then they both are laughing together in their present Boston University laboratory again."

The end of story

Printed by Libri Plureos GmbH in Hamburg,
Germany